...STER ...INGS

First published in 2014 by Wayland

Text copyright © Andrew Fusek Peters
Illustrations by Alex McArdell © Wayland

Wayland
338 Euston Road
London NW1 3BH

Wayland Australia
Level 17/207 Kent Street
Sydney, NSW 2000

Consultant: Dee Reid
Editor: Nicola Edwards
Designer: Alyssa Peacock

A CIP catalogue record for this book is available from
the British Library.

Monster savings. – (Freestylers data beast; 3)
823.9'2-dc23

ISBN: 978 0 7502 8232 1
E-book ISBN: 978 0 7502 8813 2

Printed in China

Wayland is a division of Hachette Children's Books,
an Hachette UK Company
www.hachette.co.uk

MONSTER SAVINGS

Andrew Fusek Peters
and Alex McArdell

WAYLAND
www.waylandbooks.co.uk

Freestylers

Titles in the series

Bats!

978 0 7502 8231 4

Bullies and the Beast

978 0 7502 8229 1

Monster Savings

978 0 7502 8232 1

Poison!

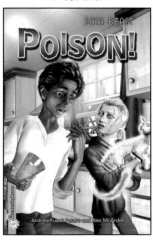

978 0 7502 8230 7

CHAPTER 1

"This place is amazing!" I whispered. "I've never seen so much stuff! I want all of it!"

The warehouse must have been a hundred foot high and the shelves seemed to go on for miles.

"Duh!" hissed Roz. "That's why it's called everythingonearth.com."

"Remind me again, why we are here?" I asked.

"This company is ripping people off," said Roz. "It doesn't pay its taxes so it makes loads of money, but there is less money for hospitals and old people."

"All this money for rich ones…" growled Data Beast.

Roz had created Data Beast on her computer. He was our pet monster made of numbers.

"Exactly!" said Roz, "and we are going to stop them."

"We need to get Data Beast inside the company's computers," Roz said. "Then we can teach them a lesson."

"But can't we do good and have a little bonus on the side?" I teased.

Roz was not in the mood for jokes.

"Kiran! If you steal any of this, I will break your fingers!" she said.

"You are as scary as Data Beast these days!" I told her.

We crept down the aisle.

"Are we near the computer centre?" I asked Data Beast.

"Yes," he said. "The hub... near now. Go up steps. See?"

We looked where Data Beast was pointing. In the middle of the vast space there was a huge round pod. There were windows on the outside. Through them we could see banks of computers.

The computer hub was empty.
Open metal stairs led up to it. We
crept towards them.

Suddenly, all the security lights went on. Then we heard a voice shout "Who's there?"

"Any clever ideas now?" I whispered to Roz.

Roz shook her head. In fact, she was shaking all over.

It was the middle of the night. We were two teenagers in a private company's warehouse. We had no escape route. We were trapped.

CHAPTER 2

Suddenly everything went dark.
Data Beast had turned off the
security lights. We stood like statues.

We heard a guard speaking on his
walkie-talkie.

"The security lights have just gone
off. They must be on the blink."

The next thing we heard was his
footsteps moving away.

Data Beast led us to the steps to the computer hub. The room was full of machines with the logo of the company shining from every screen.

"This is way in!" said Data Beast. "I go now!"

Data Beast stood up straight,
then dived into the nearest screen.

"It is so cool when he does
that!" I said.

"I just hope he will be OK," Roz
whispered.

But Data Beast wasn't OK. A
few seconds later, we heard a groan.
Data Beast appeared on the floor in
front of us. Thin smoke poured from
his mouth and his body was burned.

"Firewall hot..." he gasped.

"He needs our help," I shouted
at Roz. "What can we do?"

"I'm thinking…" Roz said.
"Have you got a USB port?" she
asked Data Beast.

Data Beast pointed to the back
of his neck.

"Right then," said Roz. "We can use numbers to heal him. Take this cable and stick it in that computer," she told me.

Roz plugged the other end into Data Beast's neck. Nothing happened.

"Come on!" she yelled at the computer.

Roz tapped at the keys until numbers flowed like a river down the screen.

"That's more like it," said Roz.

The smoke faded away. Data Beast sat up.

"I feel... better," he said.

"Nice one," I told Roz.

"Did you find what you were looking for?" Roz asked Data Beast.

"No," he said. "It was ... dead end."

Roz frowned.

"Trust me," she said. "We are going to get this company."

CHAPTER 3

The next day at school Roz said, "How about skiving off tomorrow?"

"You must be kidding!" I said. "My mum will kill me!"

"Data Beast has found out that the boss of everythingonearth.com has a big house in the country just a few hours from here," Roz told me.

"I feel a cold coming on," I said. "Looks like I won't be at school tomorrow after all."

After a train journey and a long
walk we found the house at the end of
a tiny lane. It was surrounded by high
walls, which had glass and razor wire
on top. The guards didn't look very
nice either.

"What now?" I whispered.

"Now, we break in!" said Roz.
Data Beast was hidden in the
shadows. Only his bright eyes gave
him away.

"What – we walk right in?" I asked.

"No, stupid," said Roz. "We crawl."
She pointed to a manhole cover in
the ground.

"If you think I'm crawling along
a drain to get into the house, you're
mad," I told Roz.

"Start crawling," ordered Roz.

A few minutes later, we were in the cellar. But the door in front of us was made of solid steel. In the middle of the door was keypad.

"Behind that door is a server that goes straight to the heart of the boss's evil empire," Roz said. "Every dirty data secret is hidden away."

We looked at each other.

"This is a job for Data Beast," we said.

Data Beast began to punch numbers into the keypad. Slowly at first, then so fast it was a blur. Seconds later, the massive door slid open. The room was bare except for a chair, a table, a keyboard and a screen.

I blinked and Data Beast was gone, searching through cyberspace.

Then everything happened at once. The door slammed shut, red lights flashed and alarms came on. Even worse, gas started flowing down from the ceiling.

Roz began to choke.

"We are so dead!" I cried.

CHAPTER 4

"It's knockout gas!" Roz panted.
"Hold your breath and stay low.
There has to be an off switch
somewhere."

I crawled around, feeling the floor
and under the table. Suddenly I felt a
small button on the back of one of the
table legs. I pressed it. The gas was
instantly sucked away.

"Play dead!" hissed Roz. We lay there, terrified.

A second later, the door slid open and a guard came in, talking into his walkie-talkie.

"Yeah. Couple of kids… no idea how. Out cold… Want me to deal with them? No probs."

He leaned over me. Big mistake.

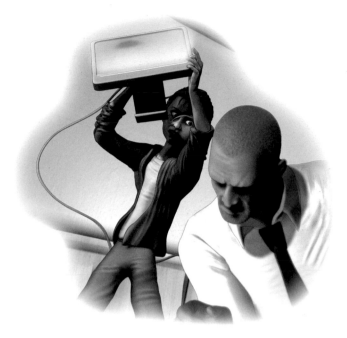

Roz ripped the monitor off the desk
and crashed it down on his head. He
crumpled.

"Let's get out of here!" she shouted
to me.

"What about Data Beast?" I asked.

"He's still in the system," Roz said.
"We will see him later!"

Back at Roz's house, we sat hunched over her laptop.

Roz's mum knocked on the door.

"Any word from Data Beast?" she asked.

Roz frowned, attacking the keys.

"Not yet," she said. "Oh… hang on a second."

Roz pointed to the screen. Data Beast was there, or rather, half there, like a bad phone signal. His mouth opened but there was no sound.

I was shocked.

"Is he…OK?" I asked Roz.

"Shh!" she said. "I'm working."

Data Beast spoke slowly.

"I went... very deep. Bots and virus, all attack me. I fight them. Found secrets. Watch news tomorrow. You will see. Now... I... feel... sad."

The picture began to fade.

"Come back!" Roz shouted. But it was no good. One by one, the numbers blinked off and bits of Data Beast whirled into cyberspace. The screen went blank. He was gone.

"Oh no. The poor thing!" Roz's mother said. She was nearly crying as she left the room.

"Data Beast can't be dead!" I cried.

"I don't know…" said Roz. There were tears in her eyes too.

CHAPTER 5

The next day Roz came to my house before school. We watched the news on her laptop. We could hardly believe what we were hearing.

On the screen was the posh boss from everythingonearth.com.

"I wish to say sorry for not paying our taxes," she said.

"From now on I have decided that it's better to be honest and to pay back all that we owe…" the boss continued.

She looked really fed up.

I grinned at Roz.

"We did it!" I said. "Even if they try to deny it later. All the data is out there. There is no going back."

Roz was trying not to cry.

"That's good," she said. "But <u>we</u> didn't do it. Data Beast did. And it cost him his life."

Suddenly Roz's computer screen started to flash. A stream of numbers flowed out and formed themselves into our favourite pet monster.

"No... not dead!" said Data Beast. "Feel alive."

Before I knew it, I was hugging
Data Beast.

I hoped Roz couldn't see the tears
in my eyes.

"Data Beast, don't you ever nearly die on us again," said Roz. Then she hugged Data Beast too.

"I like it here," said Data Beast.
"Much work to do. Find out data
secrets of all the bad guys."

"Well done, Data Beast!" I said.
"You're the beast, and you're the best!"

FOR TEACHERS

About

Freestylers is a series of carefully levelled stories, especially geared for struggling readers of both sexes. With very low reading age and high interest age, these books are humorous, fun, up-to-the-minute and edgy. Core characters provide familiarity in all of the stories, build confidence and ease pupils from one story through to the next, accelerating reading progress.

Freestylers can be used for both guided and independent reading. To make the most of the books you can:

• Focus on making each reading session successful. Talk about the text before the pupil starts reading. Introduce the characters, the storyline and any unfamiliar vocabulary.

• Encourage the pupil to talk about the book during reading and after reading. How would they have felt if they were Kiran? Or Roz? What do they think about the stand taken by Roz and Kiran against everythingonearth.com?

• Talk about which parts of the story they like best and why.

For guidance, this story has been approximately measured to:

National Curriculum Level: 2A
Reading Age: 6
Book Band: White

ATOS: 2.4
Lexile ® Measure [confirmed]: 390L